Alice in Wonderland

and

Through the Looking-Glass

Adapted for Little Folks
From the Original Story

BY
LEWIS CARROLL

With Illustrations in Full Colors from the Original Designs
by John Tenniel

BRACKEN BOOKS
LONDON

This edition published 1987 by Bracken Books
a division of Bestseller Publications Ltd
Princess House, 50 Eastcastle Street
London W1

ISBN 1 85170 109 5

Printed and bound by Times Printers, Singapore

Alice In Wonderland

ONCE upon a time there was a little girl named Alice, and she had such a funny dream. She saw a White Rabbit with pink eyes run by. He was dressed in a dear little coat and waistcoat, and he carried a tiny wee umbrella under his arm. Alice saw him take a small watch out of his pocket. Now was not that a strange thing for a little White Rabbit to do?

"Oh, dear! Oh, dear! I shall be late," she heard him say, as he looked at his watch. Now Alice had never seen a White Rabbit dressed in a coat and waistcoat before, nor had she seen one with a watch, so that when he hurried away, she jumped up and ran after him, and was just in time to see him pop down a rabbit hole.

In another moment down ran Alice after him, never thinking how she was going to get out again. It was very dark, and all at once she felt herself falling down a deep well. Down, down, down she fell through the darkness, until she thought she was never going to stop.

Then suddenly there was a thump, thump, and she found herself sitting upon a large heap of dry leaves and sticks.

Alice, who was not a bit hurt, saw in front of her the White Rabbit scurrying along. Up she jumped and ran after him again, but he turned a corner so sharply that she lost sight of him.

She looked around and found she was in a long low hall, lighted by

When Alice had opened the door she saw a long narrow tunnel. And on kneeling down she could see, at the other end, such a lovely garden. Oh! how much she wished that she could get through and pick the beautiful flowers, but the tunnel was much too small for that. It was no use wishing, so she got up, locked the door, and walked back to the little glass table again.

This time she found upon the table a small bottle on which a paper label was fastened with the words,

a row of lamps hanging from the roof. Near her was a little glass table, and on it lay a golden key.

There were doors upon each side of the hall, so Alice picked up the key and tried to open one of them, but it would not fit into any of the keyholes. Just as she was turning away she noticed a curtain, and found behind it another door that was just about large enough for a rabbit to crawl through. She tried the golden key, and was delighted to find that it fitted exactly.

"DRINK ME," printed in beautiful large letters. Alice took the cork out and tasted the contents, which was so nice that she soon drank it all up. Then such a very funny thing happened. "How curious," said Alice, "why I feel exactly like a telescope being shut up."

And so Alice was shutting up, and she went on getting smaller and smaller until she was only ten inches high. She felt very glad of this, for now she was tiny enough to run down the tunnel into that beautiful garden. She waited a few minutes to see if she would get any smaller, for at one time she thought she might shrink to nothing, and what a dreadful thing that would have been.

But as she did not shrink any more, she ran to open the little door, when, alas, she found she had left the key behind. Alice went back to the table to fetch the· key, but she had become such a tiny mite that she could not reach it. She was trying vainly to climb the slippery leg of the table when she spied a little glass box on the floor.

The box contained a small cake,

on which the words "EAT ME" were marked in currants. "I will eat it," said Alice; "if it makes me grow taller I can reach the key, and if I get smaller I can crawl under the door."

"Curiouser and curiouser!" cried Alice, forgetting to speak correctly; "now I'm opening out again like a great big telescope."

"Good-bye, feet," said Alice, for when she looked down she found that her feet were almost out of sight, they were so far off.

9

"Oh! my poor little feet, I wonder who will put your shoes and stockings on for you now, dears? I'm sure I shan't be able; you must manage the best way you can—but I must be kind to them," thought Alice, "or perhaps they won't walk the way I want."

Alice went on growing bigger and bigger, until she was twice as tall as when she ran after the White Rabbit, so of course she could very easily reach the golden key, which she hurried off with and opened the little door. Poor Alice! She began to cry bitterly when she found she was so large that she could not even get her hand into the tunnel that led into the garden.

"You ought to be ashamed of yourself," said Alice; "a great girl like you crying. Stop this moment!" But she still went on crying, until there was quite a deep pool of water all around her.

After a time she heard a pattering of feet in the distance. It was the White Rabbit returning, beautifully dressed, with a pair of white kid gloves in one hand and a large fan in the other.

He came trotting along, muttering to himself, "Oh, the Duchess! the Duchess! Won't she be angry if I keep her waiting!" As the Rabbit came nearer, Alice said in a timid voice, "If you please, sir—" but he was so frightened that he ran away, dropping his gloves and fan as he went. Alice picked up the fan and gloves, and as the hall was very hot she began to fan herself.

"I do wish somebody would come and fetch me," said Alice; then she looked down, and found that she had put on one of the Rabbit's little kid gloves. "How *could* I have done that? Why, I must be growing smaller again," she thought, as she rose and stood by the table. True enough, she was getting smaller and the cause of it was the fan with which she was fanning herself.

Alice dropped the fan quickly, but only just in time to stop herself from shrinking away altogether. "Now for the garden," she said, as she ran to the little door, but alas, she had once more left the key on the table, and could not reach it. Alice began to cry again. "It's really too bad," she sobbed. As she said this her foot slipped, and splash! she was up to her chin in salt water.

At first she thought she had fallen into the sea, and she expected to find a lot of little children with wooden shovels and pails digging in the sand, as she had done when she was once at the seaside. Alice also remembered that she went to the seaside in a train, and she thought that when she got out of the water she would be able to take the train home again.

But she soon found it was the

pool of tears she had wept when she grew so big, and not the sea at all. "I do wish I had not cried so much," said Alice, as she swam about trying to find her way out. "I shall be punished for it I expect by being drowned in my own tears. That will be a queer thing, to be sure. But everything *is* queer to-day."

Just then she heard a splashing near her, and found it was a poor little Mouse who, like herself, had slipped in. Alice thought she would ask the Mouse if he could tell her the

a queer bird called a Dodo, and three other birds, one called a Lory, one an Eaglet, and one a Duck, and many other funny animals.

Alice led the way, and the whole party swam to shore. They *were* a queer-looking lot: birds with draggled feathers, and animals with their fur all clinging to them; all were dripping wet, and all were very cross.

"The way to get dry," said the Dodo, "is for us all to have a race."

It was a very funny race. First of all, everybody was placed in a circle.

Then they ran for about half-an-hour, until all were quite dry, when the Dodo called out: "The race is over." Immediately they crowded around, asking: "Who has won?" The Dodo thought for a long time. At last he said, "Everybody has won, and all must have prizes." The Dodo said that Alice would give the prizes, and the whole party came clamoring around her.

At first Alice did not know what to do, then she felt in her pocket and found a box of sweets that the water had not hurt. Luckily, there was just one apiece.

way out. So she asked him, but he did not answer. Then she began to tell him about her cat Dinah, and what a clever mouser she was. This so frightened the poor little creature that he jumped right out of the water.

Alice said she was very sorry, and promised not to talk of cats again. So the Mouse swam back to her side, and said, "Let us get to shore." And it was quite time they did too, for the pool was getting full of no end of strange creatures. There was

"But she must have a prize herself," said the Mouse.

"Of course," said the Dodo, gravely.

"What else have you got in your pocket?" he asked.

"Only a thimble," said Alice, sadly.

"Hand it over," said the Dodo. Then he took it and solemnly presented it to her, and the animals cheered. Alice thought this very funny, but as they all looked so grave she did not dare to laugh.

Then they commenced to eat their sweets. This caused no end of noise, for the large birds complained that they could not taste theirs, and the small ones choked, and had to be patted on their backs.

After this the Mouse sat down and began to tell them a tale. In the middle of it he got up in a rage and walked away, because, he said, Alice was not listening.

Then Alice began to tell them how clever her cat Dinah was at catching mice and birds. This frightened ter, pointing with his teaspoon to the March Hare. "It was at a concert given by the Queen of Hearts, and I had to sing."

> "Twinkle, twinkle, little bat!
> How I wonder what you're at!
> Up above the world you fly,
> Like a tea-tray in the sky."

Here the Dormouse shook itself, and in its sleep began singing softly: "Twinkle, twinkle, twinkle," and went on so long that they had to pinch it to make it stop.

"I had just finished," said the Hatter, "when the Queen jumped up and shouted, 'Off with his head!'"

"Ever since then," he continued, "he won't do a thing I ask him. It's always six o'clock now."

"Is that the reason so many tea-things are put out?" asked Alice.

"Yes," replied the Hatter, sadly. "It's always tea time, and we've no time to wash up; we keep moving around."

"What happens when you come to the beginning again?" said Alice.

"Suppose we change the subject," said the March Hare.

The Dormouse was made to wake up and tell a story about three little

girls who lived on molasses at the bottom of a well.

Alice, who was very interested, asked a lot of questions about the little girls, and the March Hare was so rude that she got up and left the table. As she did so, she looked back and saw the Dormouse being dipped in the teapot.

"It's the stupidest tea-party I was ever at in my life," thought Alice, as she picked her way through the wood. Suddenly she noticed that one of the trees had a door in it, and

she was just the right size; and *then* she found herself at last in the beautiful garden among the flowers.

The roses were white, but three gardeners were busily engaged painting them red. Alice thought this so funny that she went near to watch.

"Now then, Five, look out; don't go splashing the paint over me like that," she heard one say.

"I couldn't help it," said Five; "Seven jogged my elbow."

"That's right, Five," said Seven; "always lay the blame on others."

entering, she once more found herself in the long hall and close to the glass table.

"I'll manage better this time," she said, as she took the golden key and unlocked the door that led into the garden.

Now Alice had been very careful indeed all this time to keep a bit of each side of the mushroom in her pocket, and so she set to work nibbling a bit until she was about twelve inches high. Then she walked down the little passage quite easily, for

"*You* had better not talk," said Five; "I heard the Queen say only yesterday you ought to be beheaded."

"Will you tell me," said Alice, timidly, "why you are painting those roses?"

"The fact is, Miss," said Two, in a low voice, "this ought to have been a red rose tree. We planted white in mistake, and if the Queen finds it out she'll have every one of our heads cut off."

Just then Five, who had been looking across the garden, shouted, "The Queen! The Queen!" and all the three fell on their faces.

Alice watched the long procession, anxious to see the Queen who wanted to cut everybody's head off. She saw the White Rabbit, and she saw the Knave of Hearts carrying the King's crown on a velvet cushion, and last of all came the King and Queen of Hearts.

"Who is this?" asked the Queen severely, when she saw Alice.

"My name is Alice, so please your Majesty," answered Alice. Adding to herself, "They're only cards; I needn't be afraid."

"And who are these?" said the

Queen, pointing to the three gardeners.

"How should I know?" said Alice.

The Queen turned crimson with fury. "Off with her head," she screamed.

"Consider, my dear, she's only a child," said the King.

"Can you play croquet?" shouted the Queen.

"Yes," shouted Alice.

"Come on then," roared the Queen, and Alice joined the procession.

"It's—it's a very fine day," said a timid voice at her side. She looked up and saw she was walking next to the White Rabbit.

"Very," said Alice. "Where's the Duchess?"

"Hush!" said the Rabbit.

"Her head is to be cut off for being late," he whispered.

"To your places," the Queen shouted in a voice of thunder.

People ran in all directions, but they soon began the game.

Alice had never seen such a curious croquet ground in her life; it was all hills and holes. The balls were live hedgehogs, and the mallets were funny birds with long necks, called Flamingoes.

Alice found it very difficult to play, for when she tried to strike one of the hedgehogs, her Flamingo looked up into her face, as much as to say, "What are you trying to do?" Then, when she at last did get a chance she usually found her hedgehog scampering off. Alice, who had heard the Queen order three of the players to be beheaded for missing their turns, became rather uneasy.

She was looking for a way of escape, when she saw the Cheshire Cat's head suddenly appear in the air.

"How do you like the Queen?" whispered the Cat.

"Not at all," said Alice.

"To whom are you talking?" asked the King, who came up and looked in alarm at the Cat's head.

"It's a friend of mine, a Cheshire Cat," said Alice.

"I don't like the look of it at all," said the King.

Then he asked the Queen to have the Cat's head removed.

"Off with its head," shouted the Queen.

But the Executioner said that he could not cut off a head that had no body. The Queen said if something was not done at once she would have everybody's head cut off.

"It belongs to the Duchess," said Alice.

"Then fetch her out of prison," said the Queen.

But long before the Duchess came the Cat had disappeared, and there was no head to cut off.

"I'm so glad to see you," said the Duchess, as she put her arm through Alice's.

"I give you fair warning," shouted the Queen, "either you or your head must be off; take your choice."

The Duchess took her choice and was off in a moment.

"If you have not seen the Mock Turtle yet," said the Queen, "come with me, and he shall tell you his history. They make soup of him," she explained.

As Alice went she heard the King

say: "You are all pardoned." This made her glad, for she had been quite unhappy at the thought of so many people being beheaded.

Soon they came to a Gryphon. (This is a funny animal with a bird's head and wings.)

"Take this young lady to the Mock Turtle," said the Queen, as she left.

They soon found the Mock Turtle, who looked at them with large eyes full of tears.

"Tell this young lady your history," said the Gryphon.

"Once," said the Mock Turtle with a great sigh, "I was a real Turtle."

These words were followed by a long silence, and Alice, thinking that the story was finished, said politely: "Thank you, sir, for your interesting story."

"When we were little," he continued proudly, "we went to school."

"I've been to a day school, too," said Alice; "so you need not be so proud."

"Ah! but you may not have lived much under the sea," he continued; "and, perhaps, you have never been introduced to a Lobster, and don't know what a delightful thing a Lobster Quadrille is."

"What sort of a dance is it?" said Alice.

"Form a line along the seashore," said the Gryphon.

"Two lines," said the Mock Turtle. "Seals, Turtles, and so on, each with a Lobster for a partner."

"I should very much like to see how it's done," said Alice.

So they began solemnly dancing round her, saying these words slowly and sadly:

"'Will you walk a little faster?'
    said a Whiting to a Snail,
'There's a Porpoise close behind us,
    and he's treading on my tail.
See how eagerly the Lobsters
    and the Turtles all advance!
They are waiting on the shingle,
    will you come and join the dance?'"

When they had finished dancing, the Gryphon said to Alice: "Now stand up and repeat, ''Tis the voice of the Sluggard.'" Alice was thinking so much about the quadrille that the words came very queer indeed:

"''Tis the voice of the Lobster,
    I hear him declare,
You have baked me too brown,
    I must sugar my hair!
As a Duck with its eyelids,
    so he with his nose,
Trims his belt and his buttons
    and turns out his toes.'"

"It's different from what I said when I was a child," said the Gryphon.

"I never heard it before, but it sounds very stupid," said the Mock Turtle.

Alice said nothing, but sat with her head in her hands wondering if anything would ever happen in a natural way again.

"I think you had better stop," said the Gryphon, and poor Alice was only too pleased to do so.

The Mock Turtle was just going to sing another song, when a cry was heard of, "The trial's beginning."

"Come on," cried the Gryphon and, taking Alice by the hand, it hurried her off without waiting for the end of the song.

"What trial?" Alice panted as she ran, but the Gryphon only answered, "Come on!" while more and more faintly in the distance they could hear the Mock Turtle singing.

The King and Queen of Hearts were seated on a throne with a great

29

The White Rabbit blew three blasts on his trumpet and read from the parchment as follows:

"The Queen of Hearts she made some tarts,
    All on a summer day;
  The Knave of Hearts, he stole those tarts,
    And took them quite away."

"Stupid things," began Alice, in a loud voice, but she stopped hastily, for the White Rabbit called out: "Silence in Court," and the King put on his spectacles and looked around severely to see who was talking.

"Consider your verdict," said the King to the jury, who were twelve little creatures in a box, among which were a Squirrel, a Lizard, a Frog, a Mouse, and a couple of Guinea Pigs.

"Not yet, not yet," the Rabbit interrupted; "there's a great deal more to come."

"Call the first witness, then," said the King, and the Rabbit blew three blasts, crying out: "First witness."

In came the Hatter with a teacup in one hand and a piece of bread-and-butter in the other.

crowd around them, made up of all sorts of little birds and beasts, as well as a whole pack of cards.

The Knave was standing before them in chains, with a soldier on each side to guard him.

Near the King was the White Rabbit, with a trumpet in one hand and a roll of parchment in the other.

In the middle of the Court on a table was a large dish of tarts that made Alice feel quite hungry.

"Herald, read the charge," said the King.

"I beg pardon, your Majesty," he began, "but I hadn't quite finished my tea when I was sent for."

"When did you begin?" asked the King. The Hatter looked at the March Hare who had come into Court with the Dormouse.

"Fourteenth of March, I think it was," he said.

"Fifteenth," said the March Hare.

"Sixteenth," added the Dormouse.

"Write that down and add it up," said the King to the jury.

"Take your hat off immediately," said the King.

"It isn't mine," said the Hatter; "I keep them to sell. I've none of my own," he added nervously.

"Give your evidence, and don't be nervous, or I'll have you executed on the spot," said the King.

This made the Hatter so frightened that he bit a large piece out of his teacup instead of his bread.

Just at this moment Alice felt a curious sensation; she was growing large again.

"I wish you would not squeeze so," said the Dormouse, who was next to her. "I can hardly breathe."

"Bring me the list of singers at

the last concert," said the Queen. This made the Hatter tremble so his shoes fell off.

"I'd rather finish my tea," he said.

"You may go," said the King, and the Hatter ran off so fast he forgot his shoes.

"Next," said the King.

"*Alice*," shouted the Rabbit.

"Here," cried Alice, rising, and forgetting how big she had grown, and in her hurry she upset the jury box, sending the little creatures sprawling all over the place.

"The jury must be collected again before the trial can proceed," said the King.

While the jury were being collected again the King was looking very sternly at Alice.

Suddenly he called out: "Silence." Then he read from a book: "Rule Forty-two: *All persons more than a mile high to leave the Court.*"

"*I'm* not a mile high," said Alice, as she saw everybody looking at her.

"You're nearly two miles high," said the Queen.

After Alice left a lot more witnesses were called, and then once again the King said: "Let the jury consider their verdict."

"Sentence first, verdict afterwards," said the Queen.

"Stuff and nonsense," said Alice.

"Off with her head," said the Queen.

"Who cares for you? You're only a pack of cards," said Alice. At this the whole pack rose in the air and came flying at her. She gave a little scream, and, half in fear, half in anger, was trying to beat them off, when—

She found herself lying on a bank with her head in her sister's lap.

"Wake up, Alice, dear," said her sister. "Why, what a long sleep you've had!"

"Oh! I've had such a curious dream," said Alice, and she told her sister, as well as she could remember them, all these strange Adventures of hers you have just been reading about, and truly it was a wonderful dream—was it not?

THE END OF ALICE IN WONDERLAND.

Through the Looking-Glass

Through the Looking-Glass

ONE thing was certain. The white kitten had nothing to do with it—it was the black kitten's fault entirely. For the white kitten had been having its face washed by the old cat for the last quarter of an hour. While Alice was sitting coiled up in a corner of an armchair, half asleep, the black kitten had been having a grand game of romps with a ball of worsted and had snarled it all up.

"Oh, you wicked little thing!" cried Alice, catching up the black kitten, and giving it a little kiss to make it know that it was in disgrace. "Really, Dinah ought to have taught you better manners!"

Then she scrambled back into the armchair, taking the black kitten and worsted with her, and began winding up the ball again. But she didn't get on very fast, for she kept on talking all the time either to herself or the kitten.

"Do you know what tomorrow is, Kitty?" Alice began. "You'd have guessed if you'd been at the window with me. I was watching the boys

getting sticks for the bonfire." Here Alice wound two or three turns of the worsted around the kitten's neck. That led to a scramble in which the ball rolled down upon the floor, and yards and yards of worsted got unwound again.

"Do you know I was so angry, Kitty?" Alice went on, as soon as they were comfortably settled again. "When I saw all the mischief you were doing, I was very nearly open-

"It's only the Red King snoring," said Tweedledee.

"Come and look at him!" the brothers cried, as they each took one of Alice's hands and led her to the place where the Red King was sleeping.

"Isn't he a *lovely* sight?" asked Tweedledum.

Alice couldn't say honestly that he was. He had a tall red nightcap on, with a tassel, and he was lying crumpled up into a sort of untidy heap, snoring loudly.

"What do you think he is dreaming about?" asked Tweedledee.

Alice said, "Nobody can guess that."

"Why he's dreaming about *you*, and if he left off dreaming you'd be nowhere," he said.

"You'd go bang! if he awoke," said Tweedledum.

"I shouldn't," said Alice indignantly, and she began to cry.

"Do you think it's going to rain?" inquired Tweedledum opening a large umbrella.

"It may rain outside, if it chooses. We've no objection," said Tweedledee.

"Selfish things!" thought Alice, and she was just going to say "Good-bye" and leave them, when Tweedledum sprang out from under the umbrella, and seized her by the wrist.

"Do you see that?" he asked, in a voice choking with anger, and his eyes grew large and yellow in a moment, as he pointed with a trembling finger at a small white thing lying under the tree.

"It's only a rattle," said Alice, after a careful examination of the little white thing. "Not a rattle-

new Rattle!'' and his voice rose to a perfect scream.

"Of course you agree to a battle?'' inquired Tweedledum of Tweedledee, who was trying to fold himself up in the umbrella.

"I suppose so,'' was the sulky reply, "only *she* must help us to dress up.''

So the two brothers went off hand in hand into the wood, and returned in a few minutes with their arms full of things—such as bolsters, blankets, hearth-rugs, table-cloths, dish-covers, and coal-scuttles.

"I hope you're good at pinning, and tying strings,'' remarked Tweedledum.

"Really they'll be more like bundles of old clothes than anything else,'' thought Alice, as she tied a bolster around Tweedledee's neck to keep his head from being cut off.

"You know,'' he added gravely, "it's one of the most serious things that can possibly happen to one in battle, to get one's head cut off.''

Alice laughed aloud, but managed to turn her laugh into a cough for fear of hurting his feelings.

"Do I look very pale?'' asked

snake, you know,'' she added hastily, thinking that he was frightened; "only an old rattle—old and broken.''

"I knew it was!'' cried Tweedledum, stamping about wildly and tearing his hair. "It's spoilt, of course!'' Here he looked at Tweedledee, who immediately tried to hide himself under the umbrella.

"You needn't be so angry about an old rattle,'' said Alice soothingly.

"But it isn't old! It's new, I tell you—I bought it yesterday—my nice

Tweedledum, coming to have the saucepan, which he called a helmet, tied on.

"Well—yes— a *little*," Alice replied gently.

"I've got a headache!" said Tweedledum.

"And I've got a toothache!" said Tweedledee.

"Don't fight to-day," said Alice.

"We must fight a bit, but I don't care about going on long. Suppose we fight till six o'clock and then have dinner," suggested Tweedledum. "There's only one sword," he continued, "but you can have the umbrella—it's quite as sharp. We must be quick. It's getting as dark as it can."

"It's the crow!" cried Tweedledee, in a shrill voice of alarm, and the two brothers took to their heels and were soon out of sight.

Alice ran under a large tree, for the wind was blowing hard.

"Why here's somebody's shawl being blown away," she said, and she caught it as she spoke.

In another moment the White Queen came running wildly through the wood.

"How dreadfully untidy she is," thought Alice, as she went civilly up to her and asked to be allowed to fix her up. Her hair *was* so untidy.

"The hair-brush got entangled in it," said the White Queen with a sigh.

Alice found the brush, and did her best to put her hair in order. "You look better now," she said, "but you really ought to have a lady's-maid."

"I'm sure I'll take you with pleas·

said the White Queen, "then one's memory works both ways."

"Mine only works one way," said Alice.

"That's a poor sort of memory," the White Queen remarked. "I remember things best that happened the week after next. Now, the King's Messenger—he's in prison now, being punished, and the trial doesn't even begin until next Wednesday. And, of course, the crime comes last of all."

"Suppose he never commits the

ure!" the White Queen said. "Twopence a week, and jam every other day."

Alice laughed and said, "I don't want you to hire *me*, and I don't like jam. I don't want any *to-day*, at any rate."

"You couldn't have it if you *did* want it," the White Queen said. "The rule is jam tomorrow, jam yesterday, but never to-day."

"I can't understand," said Alice. "It's dreadfully confusing!"

"Ah! you should live backwards,"

crime?" suggested Alice. "I don't see why he should be punished."

"You're wrong *there*. Were you ever punished?" asked the White Queen.

"Only for faults," said Alice.

"And it did you good, I know. Now, how old are you?" continued the White Queen.

"I'm seven and a half exactly," said Alice.

"You needn't say 'exactually,'" the White Queen remarked. "Now I'm just one hundred and one, five months and a day."

"I can't believe *that*," said Alice.

"Try again, shut your eyes, and draw a long breath," said the White Queen.

"It's no use. I can't believe impossible things," said Alice.

"You've had no practice," said the White Queen. "When I was your age, I've often believed six hundred impossible things before breakfast."

Just at this moment a gust of wind came and blew the White Queen's shawl across a little brook. The White Queen ran after it and Alice followed her.

"I've got it! I've got it!" the White

Queen cried in a triumphant tone. The last word ended in a bleat, so like a sheep that Alice was quite startled.

She looked at the White Queen, who suddenly seemed to have wrapped herself up in wool. Alice rubbed her eyes. She couldn't make out what had happened. Was she in a shop? And was that *really* a sheep that was sitting on the other side of the counter?

"What do you want to buy?" the Sheep inquired at last.

49

pen in a moment. The candles all grew up to the ceiling, the plates and cruets flew away, the soup ladle was walking upon the table towards Alice.

"I can't stand this any longer," she cried, as she seized the table cloth with both hands. One good pull, and plates, dishes, guests, and candles and all came crashing down in a heap on the floor. "And as for *you*," Alice went on, turning fiercely on the Red Queen, whom she considered the cause of all the mischief—but the Red Queen had dwindled down to the size of a little doll and was trying to escape.

"As for *you*," Alice repeated, as she caught hold of her, "I'll shake you like a kitten!"

The Red Queen made no resistance, but her face grew very small, and her eyes got very large and green. And, as Alice went on shaking her, she kept on growing shorter—and fatter—and softer—and rounder—and—, and it really *was* a kitten, after all.

"Your Red Majesty shouldn't purr so loudly," Alice said, rubbing her eyes, and addressing the kitten with some severity. Then she hugged it to show she was not really angry.

"You woke me out of—oh! such a nice dream! And you've been along with me, Kitty—all through the Looking-Glass world. Did you know it, dear?" But the kitten only purred.

THE END OF THROUGH THE LOOKING-GLASS.